ITTY & BiTTY

On the Road

written by
Nancy Carpenter Czerw

illustrated by
Rose Mary Berlin

McWITTY PRESS, New York, NY

A MINI-HISTORY

Many, many years ago, children were used to pull tubs of coal out of the mines in Great Britain. When this practice was outlawed in 1847, mine owners began to import the smallest ponies from the Shetland Islands and bred them down to a height of 34 inches, small enough to fit into the 36-inch tunnel entrances. These "pit ponies" were used in American coal mines until 1970, and the last one was retired in Britain in 1994. Today, miniature horses like Itty and Bitty provide companionship to humans by working in therapeutic riding programs, leading the blind, and comforting children and the elderly in visits to hospitals and nursing homes.

To JM-C and miles of laughter on the road with the real Itty and Bitty. —NCC
To my husband, Rick, for traveling the road with me. —RMB

www.ittyandbitty.com

ISBN 0-9755618-4-7
978-0-9755618-4-3

McWitty Press
110 Riverside Dr., 1A
New York, NY 10024
www.mcwittypress.com

They've heard of the world's great wonders—
all seven,
And one is a horse show out East known as Devon!

So they're off to the airport—
It's Devon or bust!
Even minis get a little wanderlust.

Airline passengers grouse and complain,
When flying *coach* on a crowded plane.

But Itty and Bitty just grin and know,
Coach is their favorite way to go.
For minis it could be otherwise:
Harnessed to coaches to pull twice their size,
Or hitched to carts with heavy loads—
But *here* they fly above the roads!

So they trot to their seats, grab a carrot to chew,
Strap on the headphones, and enjoy the view.

Since they can't go to Africa, they'll go to a zoo.
There's one in New York, in the Bronx, that will do.

So they take a small detour and spend a few days,
Exploring the sites of this jungle-like maze.

They see horses in stripes,
but no Pintos with spots,

**While leopards and cheetahs
are cats dressed in dots.**

There are wild spotted dogs
painted black, brown, and tan,

And a bird who has eyes in his tail—
that's a fan!

With every habitat he passes,
Itty thinks he might need glasses.

Pennsylvania, Tally-ho!
It's off to Devon now they go.

A horse show, a midway, a country fair—
Everything minis can dream of is there:
Champion horses in show braids and dapples,
Shops selling tee shirts and caramel apples.

There are hunters and jumpers and ponies galore,

Clydesdales as tall as a castle door!

Itty goes shopping for a herringbone vest.
(He spied a fine filly and must look his best!)
She's a beautiful Pinto, a lovely lass,
Who won a blue ribbon in the lead line class.

Bitty cares nothing for looking dandy.
He's off eating popcorn and cotton candy,
And riding around on the carousel—
Which horse is real? It's hard to tell!

There are coachmen in top hats and elegant coats,
Ladies in carriages, with hats big as boats.
From the top of the grandstand or Ferris wheel,
The pageant below makes a mini's head reel.

In all of the world, there is no place like Devon.
Truly, this is Horsey Heaven!

It's homeward bound, but not by ground,
For our minis, I and B.
From the Port of New York to Galveston,
This time they'll go by sea.

A cruise ship is a marvelous stable:
Eat all that you can, then more if you're able!

There are mini-cabins, mini-bunks,
Mini-showers and mini-trunks.
Swim in the pool instead of a pond;
Avoid the slimy frog and frond.

When Itty hears it's time to dance,
He puts on a tux and begins to prance.
Bitty plays bingo then eats some more,
'Til he barely fits through the cabin door!

While **Bitty** snores, **Itty** slips away,
For one last bite at the midnight buffet.

When our minis arrive on the Texas shore,
They're not so *mini* anymore!